Red and the Pumpkins

By Jocelyn Stevenson
Pictures by Kelly Oechsli

Muppet Press
Holt, Rinehart and Winston
New York

Published by Holt, Rinehart and Winston,
383 Madison Avenue, New York, New York 10017.

Library of Congress Cataloging in Publication Data
Stevenson, Jocelyn.
Red and the pumpkins.

Summary: Hoping to make life easier for all the
Fraggles, Red steals and plants a pumpkin seed from
the Gorgs' Garden—but a horrible nightmare ensues.
[1. Pumpkin—Fiction]   I. Oechsli, Kelly, ill.
II. Title.
PZ7.S8476Re 1983   [Fic]   83–10801
ISBN 0-03-068679-2
First Edition

Printed in the United States of America
1 3 5 7 9 10 8 6 4 2

ISBN 0-03-068679-2

Contents

A Plan Is Born

RED Fraggle zigzagged around the Fraggle pool, using her tail as a propeller, keeping her hands and feet free. This was one of her better tricks and she loved to show it off, especially to her friend Gobo.

"Hey, Gobo, look!" she yelled. "I've got my eyes closed!" Red covered her eyes and promptly banged into the side of the pool. "Ow!" she said, rubbing the top of her head. "Don't worry! That was part of the trick. Wasn't it great?"

But Gobo hadn't noticed. Fortunately, he was too busy executing a double backward spiral dive off the highest rock. Red sighed with relief; she hated to have anyone see her make a mistake. She leaned back and watched a large radish settle down above her at the edge of the pool.

"Hi, Mokey!" Red said. "Just back from the Garden?"

Mokey Fraggle emerged from behind the radish. Her pink face was streaked with mud, and the comfortable old sweater she always wore was ripped and unraveling.

"Yes," Mokey said, sitting down to cool her toes in the water. "But that Gorg almost got me this time!"

"Oh, Mokey, you look awful!" Red exclaimed, pulling herself out of the pool. "What happened?"

Red had never understood how her gentle friend could go to the Gorgs' Garden to gather vegetables for the Fraggles. The Gorgs were giants—fifteen times the size of Fraggles—and they were horrible. All they wanted to do with Fraggles was chase and thump them. Even so, for as long as five minutes a day, Mokey risked her life in the Gorgs' Garden.

"Most of the time it's really easy," said Mokey dreamily. "But sometimes, like today, I sort of wish that radishes weren't so hard to carry. The problem isn't picking them; the problem is getting them back to the Rock in a hurry."

"Isn't there anything in the Garden besides radishes?" asked Red.

"Oh, yes," said Mokey. "There're turnips and onions and potatoes and tomatoes and lettuce and pumpkins and—"

"Pumpkins? What are pumpkins?" asked Red. She liked the sound of the word.

"Oh, pumpkins are great big beautiful round orange things. They look delicious, but they're way too enormous to bring back to the Rock. It's a shame; a pumpkin would last a lot longer around here than a radish." To prove her point, Mokey nodded toward the spot where the radish had been. It had vanished and four satisfied Fraggles were resting on the ground.

"Thanks, Mokey!" they said. "Great radish!"

"I think we need another one, don't you?" asked Mokey, getting to her feet a little more stiffly than usual.

"Oh no!" insisted Red. "You're not going out there again. You need a break." She drew herself up responsibly. "I'll go."

"But you can't go," objected Mokey. "Gathering vegetables from the Gorgs' Garden is my job; your job is cleaning the pool."

"I'll do overtime today," Red said emphatically. "I'm going to pick a giant vegetable and I'm going now!" She turned and ran right into a stalagmite. Picking herself up, she declared, "This time I'm really going!" She zipped around the stalagmite and past another one without tripping once.

As she skipped toward the Garden, Red thought about what a great friend Mokey was. But then Gobo, Boober, and Wembley were good friends, too. All five of them lived in Fraggle Rock, a beautiful underground world filled with caves and tunnels and thousands and thousands of Fraggles. At the center of Fraggle Rock was Red's favorite place—the huge pool where everyone swam.

But now Red had reached her least favorite place—the Gorgs' Garden. She tiptoed cautiously out of the Rock, hid behind a clump of grass, and peeked out. To her horror, she saw Junior Gorg working nearby, right in front of the crumbling castle where the Gorg family lived. Red looked at him, from his size-eight-million shoes to the top of his shaggy brown head, and gulped. He was talking to himself and she could just make out the words.

"Those little Fraggles took another one of my radishes," he said, shaking his giant fist. "But never again. No sirree! Next time, I'll get them first!"

Peeking through the grass, Red saw that Junior had moved to the other end of the Garden. She decided it was safe and stuck out one foot, then the other. She was about to race to the nearest row of vegetables when the door to the dilapidated castle swung open and Pa Gorg, Junior's father and self-proclaimed King of the Universe, swaggered out. He was wearing a helmet and carrying a shield—always prepared for battle even though there was never anyone to fight.

"Junior!" he bawled.

"Oh, please don't holler and yell, King Daddy," begged Junior. "I didn't mean to let the Fraggles get a radish, they just took it and—"

Pa raised his hand for silence. He slowly marched up and down the twenty-two rows of radishes Junior had planted.

"Junior, my son, you've got too many radishes here," announced Pa. "And too many radishes give me indigestion. I want you to plant something else."

"Are you sure?" asked Junior disappointedly. He planted radishes because he knew Fraggles liked them, and luring Fraggles into his Garden, where he could catch them, was his favorite pastime.

"Of course I'm sure—I'm the King!" bellowed Pa. "Now, I'm going to sharpen my sword while you plant something else, and that's an order!" He toddled off into the castle to find his sword.

Junior lumbered toward the old rotting toolshed at the end of the Garden. He was so upset at having to change his plans that he didn't even notice Red scurrying along behind him.

"If King Daddy said, 'Plant something else,' then I'd better plant something else. But what?" Junior wondered. "Let's see now—where did I put those seeds?" He started hurling things out of the shed. Finally Junior shouted, "Pumpkins!"

"Oh boy, oh boy!" he cried, jumping up and down with delight. "I haven't planted pumpkins in a long time." He picked up a packet of seeds, turned it over, and stared dimly at the writing on the back. " 'With proper care, these seeds will grow into pumpkins fit for a king,' " he slowly read aloud.

Junior reached for a shovel and started digging up the ground to plant his seeds. "I hope these pumpkins are fit for a Fraggle," he said, "because then I'll get 'em! Oooo, I'd love to get me a Fraggle!"

Just thinking about Fraggles made him dig faster; while he was distracted, Red sneaked farther into the Garden and hid behind a cabbage. Suddenly, Junior threw down his shovel. The ground heaved under Red's feet, and she grabbed a leaf to steady herself.

"Planting sure is hard work," the Gorg mumbled, wiping his massive, matted brow. "Almost done now, though!" He picked up his packet of seeds and shook it.

"Are you ready, little pumpkin seeds?" he chuckled. He poured the seeds into his hand. "Now, I want all of you to grow as fast as you can into delicious big pumpkins for Ma and Pa. And don't worry about Fraggles!" Junior looked warily around the Garden. Red flattened herself against the cabbage leaf and held her breath. Junior relaxed, but as he turned to drop the seeds into the ground, he tripped over the shovel, and the seeds flew out of his hands and scattered all over the place. The packet and a seed landed near Red's left foot.

"Now look what you've done, Mr. Shovel!" Junior scolded. "You made my seeds run away!" Crawling on his hands and knees, he picked the seeds out of the dirt and put them in his pocket. As he got closer and closer to the seed by Red's foot, she could practically feel his hot breath on her orange fur. She shuddered; another few steps and he'd be right on top of her!

Red glanced at the picture on the seed packet. "That must be what a pumpkin looks like!" she whispered to herself. "Mokey's right—it's beautiful!" Red looked at the Gorg, then at the seed. She felt the tingling in her hands, feet, and the tip of her nose that she always felt when she was on the verge of A Great Plan. Quick as a wink, she grabbed the seed and ran toward the tunnel that led to Fraggle Rock.

Junior glanced up and saw a seed with legs running across the Garden. "Huh?" he exclaimed. Then he glimpsed Red's tail and recognized her for what she was. "Fraggle!" he roared, lunging after her. "Give me my pumpkin seed!"

Gasping for breath, Red dove into the Rock, just as Junior's hand closed over the entrance, blocking the light.

Red groped for the seed and pushed it toward the wall. She collapsed on top of it, relieved to be out of all that terrible open space. She waited for her heart to slow down and her chest to stop heaving. Suddenly, Junior's huge hairy fingers reached in, searching the mouth of the tunnel.

"Don't take that seed, little Fraggle. It's not a pumpkin yet!" The Gorg's voice echoed through the tunnel and boomed in Red's ears. "Give it back and I'll grow it into a pumpkin bigger than any pumpkin you could ever dream of!"

"That's what you think," Red said to herself.

She cowered against the rock wall. One of the Gorg's fingers brushed the tip of her fiery red hair, but she was safe.

2

Sneaking in the Seed

RED kept her head down until Junior Gorg's thundering footsteps stopped shaking the tunnel floor. Then she slowly sat up and brushed herself off.

"How can Mokey face that horrible monster day in and day out, and never once get caught in the Garden?" she wondered. She studied the seed lying in the dirt beside her. "Well, she won't have to worry about Gorgs anymore because I've got a Plan!" Red paced the tunnel. "I'm going to plant you, seed! Then you can grow into a giant pumpkin right here in Fraggle Rock." Red was so excited she jumped up and down, almost knocking her head on the rocky ceiling. "We won't ever have to go to the Gorgs' Garden again! It's a fantastic Plan—the best Plan I've had in a long time!"

Red loved to make Plans, but sometimes they didn't work

out exactly as she hoped. She always felt embarrassed when that happened—even though her friends would never laugh at her, she still hated to admit she'd failed at anything. So she didn't want to take any chances this time. "I think I'll keep you a secret," Red whispered to the seed. "When you grow into a beautiful pumpkin, it'll be a wonderful surprise! But if you don't grow, well, we won't be embarrassed—because no one will know."

Red hid the seed under her sweater. Though the bottom stuck out and got mixed up with her legs and the top jabbed her in the chin when she ran, she still thought it was a good place to hide it. She made her way carefully through the tunnel toward the Great Hall, which was the center of activity in Fraggle Rock. There she stopped. She needed to map her route carefully; if any Fraggles saw her with a pumpkin seed sticking out of her sweater, they might suspect something. Her secret would be out. Hiding in the shadows, she watched as Gobo prepared to plunge into the pool.

"Last one in's a fuzzball!" he shouted gleefully as he jumped.

Instantly the water was frothy with Fraggles of all sizes and colors diving in from all directions. A few dozen Fraggles leaped off the high rocks, ten or twenty more somersaulted down the slide, and a couple of Elder Fraggles swung from opposite sides of the Great Hall on two long vines. They crashed head-on and slithered into the Fraggle pool, cackling. Red watched them all admiringly, thinking how much fun it was to be a Fraggle.

Wembley Fraggle stood at the edge of the water, trying to decide whether to plop in or not. Wembley always had a hard time making decisions. Red knew that every day was a trial for her little green friend—he couldn't even decide which of his two shirts to wear, though both of them were exactly the same.

"Wembley, don't jump!" cautioned Boober Fraggle, who was crossing the Hall with an armload of wet socks. "I wouldn't dive in there for a million pebbles. Don't you know that water sticks to your fur? It can cause all sorts of terrible problems. For instance, it gives you—"

"Wet fur," said Gobo, spouting water.

Boober shook his head. "I'm warning you," he said. Boober was always warning somebody about something. "You'll be sorry!" he added, plodding off before his friends could turn the whole incident into a joke. Boober hated jokes.

From her spot close to the wall, Red had heard Boober's warning. Although he was one of her best friends, Red found Boober's glumness hard to take. She was a very positive sort of Fraggle, and she was very positive that Boober was too negative.

Red clutched her seed tighter and ducked behind a boulder. All through the Great Hall, Fraggles teeter-tottered, wrestled, skipped, hopped, tumbled, leaped, and danced. They laughed, sang, whooped, whistled, and yodeled. Red passed Mokey, who was serenely painting a flower on a big orange balloon. Mokey was so involved in her picture, she didn't see Red skulking past a nearby rock pile. Red eased around the gently wafting mound of balloons surrounding Mokey and continued through the Great Hall.

Though the Hall was huge, Red managed to make it unseen to the Fire Station. She kept close to the wall, where the shadows made her practically invisible, and had almost

reached the other end of the cave when she tripped on her
long tail and knocked over a Doozer suspension bridge. It fell
to the ground with a tinkling crash. Red ducked into a crev-
ice, but fortunately no one but the Doozers noticed that anything had happened. They deftly avoided the crash without
so much as a skewed helmet, then calmly marched back in
to resume work. Doozers, who were knee-high to Fraggles,
spent all their time building bridges and monuments and tow-
ers and anything else they could dream up. Fraggles loved
the Doozer constructions—they ate them as fast as the Doozers built them!

Popping a Doozer stick into her mouth, Red made it safely
to the other side of the Hall. She zipped into the tunnel that

went past Gobo and Wembley's room and peeped in the window. No one was there.

"I need to find something to dig with," she told her seed. "That's Phase One of my Plan."

She ran into the room and looked through Gobo's stuff. In his big rock chest, she found the perfect tool—a spoon.

"Aha!" she cried triumphantly. "A digger! Now Phase Two—find a place to dig!" Red knotted the end of her tail around the spoon, tucked the seed back under her arm and, carefully looking in both directions, crept back into the tunnel.

3
Gardening Isn't Easy

As Red made her way farther and farther away from the bustle of the Great Hall, the tunnels became darker and darker, and quieter and quieter. Damp, musty air, smelling like the inside of an old hat, closed in on her. Occasionally a cave or tunnel was lit by the eerie green glow of cragbugs, but most were pitch-black. When Red stopped to rest—the pumpkin seed got heavier with every step—she heard the soft whir of boulder bats and the slithery hiss of rocksnakes. Red didn't stop much.

"Don't worry," she assured her seed. "I'll find someplace nice to plant you. It just has to be far away so we can keep you a secret." A boulder bat flew by, flapping its wings close to Red's tousled hair.

"Let's get out of here," she gulped, quickening her pace.

She made sure the knot in her tail was still secure around the digger and headed for a pin of light in the distance. As she approached, the pin turned into a button that turned into a plate that got bigger and bigger until it turned into the mouth of a small cave. Red cautiously peeked in. Light filtered through cracks in the ceiling, making the small room almost friendly. Other than a few harmless flicker flies, no one seemed to live there. Red liked the place.

"Well, seed," she said happily, "we've found your new home!" Red untied the knot in her tail and put the seed down. "I'll call this 'Pumpkin Cave'! Now for Phase Three!" and she started digging.

The ground was surprisingly soft and moist, so it didn't take her long to make a good-sized hole in the center of the cave. She leaned the digger against the wall, carefully placed the seed in the hole, and covered it with dirt.

"Okay, seed, consider yourself planted." She sat beside the hole. "I've done my part, now you do yours."

Not knowing anything about how seeds turn into plants, Red naturally thought she'd have instant pumpkins. Instead, the seed just lay there.

"All right, seed! It's time for Phase Four! Grow into a pumpkin, please." Red thought maybe it needed a little encouragement.

Still nothing happened.

"Come on, I haven't got all day!" Red waited another long moment and then whispered, "Please, seed, don't let me down. I'm counting on you."

Still the seed just lay there, stubbornly doing nothing, least of all turning into a pumpkin.

"I guess Phase Four's going to take longer than I thought," Red sighed.

Her stomach growled, and she suddenly remembered she hadn't had anything to eat all day except a bite of a Doozer bridge. Since it looked like she wasn't going to gorge on delicious pumpkin, she decided to go back and eat a nice tower or something.

"What you need is a good rest—right, seed?" she said, deciding the seed was probably too tired to grow. "You've had a long, exciting day. I'll nip back, have a bite to eat, play with my friends, and then burrow in for the night. I'll see you tomorrow, okay?"

Red waved good-bye to her pumpkin seed and skipped back to Gobo and Wembley's room, where she put the spoon back in Gobo's rock chest without anyone seeing her.

The next day, when Gobo and Wembley were exploring the Northeast Ravine, and Mokey was painting more balloons, and Boober was reading his book of superstitions, Red slipped off to Pumpkin Cave to check on her seed.

When she arrived, she was disappointed to find that the place where she'd planted the seed looked exactly the same as it had the day before. Red wasn't the sort of Fraggle to abandon a Plan, but she was losing her patience fast. Normally, if nothing happened in the flick of a tail, Red, like any healthy fuzz-blooded Fraggle, went on to something else. But this time, she decided to wait it out. She really wanted this Plan to work. She figured if the seed never grew, no one, not even Gobo, would know she had failed. But if it did grow, everyone would have pumpkins. No more trips to the Gorgs' Garden!

"Okay, seed, I'll wait," she sighed. "You stay where you are and I'll come see you tomorrow."

Red came back the next day; still no change. And she came back the next—still nothing. She was getting depressed, discouraged, and worried.

"Listen, seed," she said, "you're doing something you shouldn't do—you're making me mad! So shape up and grow! Please! You don't want my Plan to fail, do you? Please, please grow into a yummy pumpkin."

She stomped out of the cave. The whole thing put her in a bad mood, but she thought a dip in the pool just might cheer her up. As she headed back to the Great Hall, she realized how hard it was to have a secret Plan, especially if it didn't work.

"I don't get it," Red fumed. "If pumpkins grow in the Gorgs' Garden, why not here? Fraggle Rock is a great place to grow. I bet that old seed's just lazy. I bet it doesn't even—"

"Hey, watch it!" cried Boober as Red banged right into him and sent his laundry flying. "Those socks were clean," he groaned. "Now I'll have to start all over again."

Doing the laundry was Boober's job (just as cleaning the pool was Red's and gathering radishes was Mokey's). All Fraggles had jobs and were expected to put in a good thirty minutes working every week. That left everyone plenty of time to play, so nobody minded having jobs much. Boober actually liked his. But Boober generally liked things that others didn't like and didn't like things that everyone else did. That's why he irritated Red so much.

"Sorry, Boober, but—" Red began.

"You just don't understand," he moaned. "If it weren't for

me, this place would be filled with dirty socks."

"If it weren't for you," said Red evenly, "there wouldn't be any dirty socks. You're the only one who wears socks."

Boober pulled his hat farther down over his eyes. This discussion was going nowhere. No one would ever understand about laundry, no matter how hard he tried. He opened his mouth to make another point, but Red stopped him.

"I don't want to talk about it. I've had a bad day." She paused, then added, "A very bad day."

Boober quickly picked up his socks. Red-on-a-bad-day was too much for a sensitive—and easily terrified—Fraggle like Boober. He was glad to see Gobo, Wembley, and Mokey running toward them, playing tag.

"Hey, Gobo! We're over here!" he called, desperately hoping they could help cheer up Red. Gobo, Mokey, Wembley, Boober, and Red had known each other forever. They stuck together through Red's Plans and Gobo's adventures, through Mokey's fantasies and Boober's depressions. They even helped Wembley decide which shirt to wear. They were very good friends.

"Hi, Boober!" said Gobo. "What's up?"

"Ahem," said Boober, pointing meaningfully at Red.

"A hem?" asked Mokey. "No, Boober, a hem is down. See?" She patiently showed him the bottom edge of Red's sweater.

"Mokey," interrupted Boober, "I didn't say 'a hem,' I said 'ahem'!"

"He was clearing his throat," explained Gobo.

"And pointing at Red," Wembley added.

Red eyed Boober suspiciously, and he suddenly felt slightly

uncomfortable. He had to think quickly—the last thing he wanted Red to know was that he was trying to cheer her up.

"No, Wembley, you've got it all wrong," he said. "I was pointing at Red and saying 'ahem' because . . . because . . . um, saying 'ahem' while pointing at someone nice with red hair is very lucky."

"It is?" said Mokey. She was interested in Boober's superstitions. "Why?"

"Why? Ah, good question," stalled Boober. "I mean, it . . . er . . . keeps dreams away!" And Boober started chanting "ahem" over and over again while pointing frantically at Red.

"But Boober, why would anyone want to keep dreams away?" asked Mokey innocently. "Dreams are nice, aren't they?"

"Not if they're nightmares," said Boober, his voice cracking with anxiety.

"Now, I guess that's true . . ." said Mokey, and she, Gobo, and Wembley finally joined in, much to Boober's relief. Soon the entire population of Fraggle Rock picked up the rhythm and bounced around chanting "ahemahemahem" while gaily pointing at Red. The Great Hall rumbled with so many "ahems" that it sounded like it was full of rolling rocks. Everyone thought it was lots of fun, especially Red. Being the center of attention always pleased her, and this time it took her mind off her worrisome Plan.

Soon the Fraggles tired of pointing at Red and saying "ahem," so they went back to swimming or yo-yoing or rock sliding or tossing around Mokey's painted balloons or whatever else they felt like doing.

Mokey, Gobo, Boober, and Wembley sprawled on the ground next to Red.

"Whew! That was fun!" said Mokey, fanning her face.

"Sure was," agreed Gobo. "You know, this is the first time we've played together in days, Red. Where have you been?"

"Yes, you know we haven't really seen you since that day when the Gorg almost caught me," said Mokey wistfully.

"And I've got six new sparkly rocks to show you," said Wembley. He scratched his fuzzy green head. "I can't decide which ones to keep."

Red struggled to find a convincing answer. "Well . . . er . . . I've been looking for my . . . er . . . my ribbon, the long green one with the orange polka dots. Anybody seen it?" Red felt her answer wasn't as smooth as it could have been.

"Is something wrong, Red?" Mokey asked.

"Oh no, Mokey," Red answered as calmly as she could.

"You shouldn't worry about things, you know," said Mokey. "I find they always end up working out okay, so why bother to worry?"

But Red was worried, and she was finding it increasingly difficult to keep her Plan a secret, particularly from Mokey. Once she'd almost started a casual conversation about how plants grow, to see if she could pick up a few tips from her best friend. But she decided that Mokey probably didn't know, and if she did, she'd ask so many questions that the secret would escape for sure.

Unlike the seed, the secret had grown so big that Red could barely keep it to herself anymore. It tumbled around inside her, bursting to get out. Red was dying to tell Mokey, but not as much as she was dying to show off that very first pumpkin.

Of course, there was the possibility—however remote— that the seed might never grow at all, and the whole Plan might fail. No, it was taking a little longer than Red thought it would, but that seed was bound to grow.

"I'm hungry," said Gobo. "Let's race to the Pantry!"

Red couldn't resist racing Gobo, Plan or no Plan. "Last one there is a fuzzball!" she yelled, and dashed off, leaving her worries about the seed behind her.

4

Success at Last

THE next day, Red couldn't sneak off to Pumpkin Cave until long after lunch. She had decided that if nothing happened by then, she would give up. After all, it had been nearly six days since she completed Phase Three, and she was feeling very discouraged.

"Okay, seed, this is your last chance," she said, entering the cave. "Please don't let me down." Taking a deep breath and holding her tail for luck, she looked into the hole.

"Whoooooopeeeeeee!!!"

The seed had sprouted! It was growing! Soon there would be a pumpkin in Fraggle Rock!

Red gave herself a big hug—partly because she felt she deserved it, and partly because she was the only one around. Then she raced back through the tunnels, tiptoed past Gobo and Wembley's room, and charged into the little cave she shared with Mokey. She swept her sweaters, Fraggle racket, yo-yo, pebbles, and wrinkled ribbons off the bed and climbed in. She couldn't wait to get to sleep. The sooner she finished today, the sooner she could start tomorrow and Phase Five of her Plan.

But sleep wouldn't come; every time Red closed her eyes, they popped open. She tried thinking quiet thoughts, but all she could think about were pumpkins. She tried counting Doozers, but in her mind they kept turning into fat little pumpkins. She finally tried putting her head under the covers, but it was no use. She was just too excited to sleep. "Maybe Boober was right," sighed Red. "Maybe all that 'ahemahemahem' stuff does keep dreams away."

After tossing and turning for a long time, Red heard Mokey coming down the tunnel toward their room, singing a little bedtime song. Red propped herself up on her elbow. "Hi, Mokey."

"Are you burrowed in already?" Mokey was surprised. Red was usually the last one to go to bed.

"Yes, but I can't go to sleep," grumbled Red, sitting up. "Do you think saying 'ahem' while pointing at someone with red hair really does keep dreams away? I haven't had one for a long time."

"I doubt it," laughed Mokey. "If you really want to know, Boober only did that to make you feel better."

"So he just made it up?" asked Red, relieved.

"I think so," answered Mokey. "Were you worried about not having a dream tonight?"

"Oh, not really," fibbed Red. "I'd just hate to think that one of Boober's stupid superstitions really worked, that's all."

She lay back and stared at the ceiling. Of course she wanted to dream, tonight more than ever. Dreaming was one of the best things a Fraggle could do. For Fraggles, the dream world was the second greatest place to play, next to the real world in Fraggle Rock. And everyone knew that if you could dream a dream long enough, you could make it come true.

Mokey hummed softly as she got ready for bed, and Red, lulled by the gentle tune, started to drift to sleep. She turned toward the wall and pulled the covers over her head.

"It's time to dream that my seed turns into a pumpkin," she thought sleepily.

5

Hurray for Red!

THE next thing Red knew it was dawn. She eased quietly out of bed and pulled a sweater on over her head. Being careful not to wake Mokey, she found a candle and slipped out of the room. An eerie blue mist covered everything. This was the strangest dawn Red had ever seen—hauntingly quiet.

At first Red couldn't seem to make her feet move. But she was so eager to get to Pumpkin Cave that she willed herself to put one foot in front of the other. Once she got going, she floated effortlessly through the tunnel, across the Great Hall, and along the dark passage. When she saw the mouth of her secret cave, Red was so nervous she could barely keep her candle still.

Holding her breath to control her trembling, she crept to

the spot where she'd planted the seed. It was gone! In its place was a beautiful baby pumpkin!

"This is it!" she shouted. "My Great Plan worked!"

Red hopped around the cave, ecstatic. "No more trips to the Gorgs' Garden! Let's hear it for the seed! Let's hear it for pumpkins! Let's hear it for Red Fraggle!"

Red pushed the pumpkin out of the cave and through the winding tunnels. To her surprise, it was light as a feather! The blue mist still wafted around her feet, but by the time she got to the Great Hall, Doozers were beginning to work, and some Fraggles were just coming out of their caves. Red parked the pumpkin next to the pool and clambered up the rock that supported the giant Fragglehorn. "I'm going to call a meeting!" she crowed happily. "Wait until everyone hears what I've done—they won't believe it!"

Standing on tiptoe to reach the blowing end of the Fragglehorn, she cupped her hands around the small hole and blew. The blaring honk was music to a Fraggle's ears. Each and every one of them dropped whatever he or she was doing and headed for the Great Hall.

"Whoopee! A meeting!" they cried, floating in from all directions. "Fragglefragglefragglefragglefraggle!"

Red watched the gathering throng with delight. Her big moment had finally arrived. Phase Five! She saw Gobo, Wembley, Mokey, and Boober near the pool.

"Hey Red, what's up?" yelled Gobo.

Red solemnly raised her hands for silence. She didn't get it. "QUIET!" she yelled. The only sound was the hum of the Doozer machines.

"Fellow Fraggles," she proclaimed, "I have called you here

to give you a wonderful surprise!" Red proudly pointed to her pumpkin. "That, my friends, is a pumpkin!"

"Ooooooooohhhh!"

"I grew it right here in Fraggle Rock!" she added, so pleased with herself she could barely stand it. "No more trips to the Gorgs' Garden!"

The Fraggles' cheers were deafening.

"Go ahead, taste it!" Red insisted.

A few Fraggles, including Wembley, tried to bite into the pumpkin.

"We can't eat that, Red!" Wembley said, rubbing his jaw. "It's too hard."

"According to my book on superstitions," warned Boober, "round orange things are bad luck and hard round orange things which come as surprises are even worse!"

But Red was not discouraged. And sure enough, her problem was solved by two Elder Fraggles perched on rocks on opposite sides of the hall overhead. "Ready, Homer?" yelled one of them. "Let's do it, Lyle," shouted the other. And then each of them grabbed a vine, swung over, and crashed into the pumpkin. It split with a loud "WHACK!," revealing the juiciest, most scrumptious food ever tasted in Fraggle Rock.

The Fraggles nearest the pumpkin grabbed what they could and gobbled it up, spitting out the seeds. Even Boober put down his book to give it a try.

"Delicious!" said Gobo, who'd eaten a large handful.

"Hurray for pumpkins!" cried Red's friends.

"Hurray for Red!" cried all the Fraggles. "The Pumpkin Queen!"

Red was the happiest Fraggle in Fraggle Rock.

6

Pumpkins on Parade

"WE want pumpkin! We want pumpkin!" shouted the hungry Fraggles.

"Hold your tails, there's more where that came from!" cried Red triumphantly. She slid down the rock and ran across the Great Hall.

"Where're you going, Red?" shouted Gobo as she whizzed past. She slowed for a second, then decided she still wanted to keep her cave a secret. She wanted to be Pumpkin Queen just a little while longer.

"I'll tell you later!" she called as she sprinted toward Pumpkin Cave. Once out of sight, she stopped to catch her breath. "Gosh, I don't even want to think about what I'll do if there are no more pumpkins there," she thought. Then she ran on, the cries of "Pumpkin! Pumpkin!" fading behind her.

When Red reached her secret cave, she discovered, with great relief, not one, but six more pumpkins, all attached to a long, green vine that seemed to grow longer by the second.

She sighed happily and wiped her forehead with the tip of her furry tail. "All that worrying for nothing!" she giggled gratefully. Mokey was right. Things do end up working out okay. And this was even more than okay! Red pulled the nearest pumpkin off the vine and rolled it back to the Great Hall.

Dozens of ravenous Fraggles ate the delicious pumpkin in dozens of ravenous gulps—one gulp each. The pumpkin's shell, relieved so suddenly of its contents, collapsed like a deflated balloon. One of the Fraggles picked it up, wadded it into a tiny ball, and passed it to the Fraggle next to her.

"Let's play Pass the Pumpkin!" she cried.

Everyone whooped and cheered as the pumpkin shell passed quickly from Fraggle to Fraggle.

"This is the best dream I've been in in a long time," someone giggled.

"Who says it's a dream?" asked Red.

But no one heard her. "Pumpkins!" they yelled.

Red thought they should give her a few seconds to catch her breath, but she wasn't one to complain when she saw how much fun her friends were having. Besides, being the brilliant Fraggle behind a brilliant Plan was bound to have its drawbacks. Not being able to play when you wanted to was obviously one of them.

Refreshed by joyful whoops and hollers and half a Doozer bridge, Red whizzed back to Pumpkin Cave. This time she was greeted with twenty pumpkins. The vine had twisted

elegantly around the cave and was headed for the opening.
Red couldn't believe her luck, though she preferred to think
of it as skill.

"Who needs the Gorgs' Garden when you've got a Red
Fraggle?" she congratulated herself.

She picked the biggest pumpkin and rolled it back to the
Great Hall. As she approached the entrance, she thought she
heard Wembley whisper, "Here she comes!" So when she
shoved the pumpkin into the Hall, she wasn't entirely surprised when the Fraggles sang the official Fraggle Fanfare in
her honor.

"Wibba, wobba, weeba, woo! Good for us and GOOD
FOR YOU! Whoopee!" And they threw pumpkin seeds like
confetti.

As the last notes of the ancient and sacred chant faded,
Red's heart swelled with pride.

"My fellow Fraggles," she began, brushing a tear from her
eye. "I'm honored—"

"Pumpkins! Pumpkins!" shouted the joyful crowd. They
had no time for speeches.

Red sighed; her Plan was wearing her out. She spent all
her time racing to and from Pumpkin Cave and didn't have
any time to play with her friends. She was about to ask Mokey
and Gobo for help when she noticed something very unex-
pected. She blinked and looked again, but there was no mistake. The seeds the Fraggles had tossed were sprouting. They
were growing into pumpkins! Red was flabbergasted. What
had taken her seed days and days to do, these seeds did in
no time flat!

She picked up a pumpkin, scooped out the seeds, and threw

them gleefully into the crowd. The moment they touched the ground, they sprouted. Actually, the moment they touched anything, they sprouted. Red noticed a few Fraggles growing pumpkins in their hats, and Gobo had one coming out of his back pocket.

Mokey rushed up to Red and threw her arms around her friend. "You're so wonderful! I'll never have to see those horrible Gorgs again. We'll have pumpkins forever!"

She picked up a stunningly beautiful pumpkin that had grown next to her foot. "I'll paint this one just for you!" she cried and ran off.

By this time, the Fraggles were going wild. Wagging their

tails and smacking their lips, they picked pumpkins as fast as
they grew. And the pumpkins kept growing—the more pumpkins, the more seeds; the more seeds, the more pumpkins.

"Yippee!" cried Red, tumbling around the Great Hall and
joining in the games. "Now we have our own Gorgs' Garden
to play in—without the Gorgs!"

She and her friends played Catch the Pumpkin, King (or
Queen) of the Pumpkin, Ring Around the Pumpkin, Juggle
the Pumpkin, and then Catch the Pumpkin again to work
up an appetite. After they played Eat the Pumpkin, Red
invented a game called "Squash." Anyone could play—all a
Fraggle had to do was jump from a high rock and land on a

pumpkin. It wasn't difficult; the Hall was rapidly filling up with pumpkins. They kept growing and growing; there were pumpkin vines loaded with big fat pumpkins everywhere!

A surge of Fraggles lined up behind Red to play Squash. She selected a pumpkin and was just about to break the squashing record when she noticed that the vine from Pumpkin Cave had grown right into the Great Hall. She watched as it slowly snaked along the edge of the Hall, sprouting pumpkins like orange bubbles out of a bubble pipe. It was the most glorious thing she had ever seen.

As the vine pushed through the frolicking Fraggles, they clambered on top for a ride. Riding the big green vine was more fun than a triple sideways somersault down the slide!

And still the pumpkins kept growing.

Red looked down and decided that it would be more challenging to try *not* to squash a pumpkin. She jumped. Her aim was perfect—she landed with a soft thud right between two great big pumpkins. She was heading for the ladder to try it again when she noticed that the larger of the two pumpkins was slowly, steadily moving toward her.

"Nice try, Gobo," she giggled, assuming that he was behind it.

She hid, waiting to ambush Gobo as he pushed the pumpkin past. The pumpkin rolled by and Red leaped out.

"Got you!" she cried triumphantly.

But there was no one there.

The pumpkin rolled on all by itself, and as it bumped over the floor of the Great Hall, it made an awful "ahemahema-hemahem" sound.

"What . . . ?" Puzzled, Red looked around. It wasn't just

that one pumpkin; all the pumpkins had started to move on their own. They rolled around, jockeying for space.

At first, the Fraggles laughed and ran away, thinking that Pumpkin Tag was a great game. But they soon realized there was no longer anywhere to run. There were pumpkins all over the place, sprouting and growing. And the vine kept getting longer and longer, moving faster and faster. It wrapped itself around stalagmites and twisted its way through the Fire Station and the Trading Post; now Red could see that it was about to attack the Yo-Yo Emporium. Everywhere the vine went, it left larger and larger pumpkins that chased Fraggles, rumbling "ahemahemahemahem. . . ."

Pretty soon there were more pumpkins in Fraggle Rock than Fraggles.

Gobo shook off the pumpkin shell he had been wearing on his head. "Hey Red, it's getting a little crowded in here," he said as nicely as he could. "How about saving the rest of the pumpkins for later?"

"Later?" Red said vaguely. She grinned and danced around a pumpkin to hide her growing panic. "But I'm having so much fun now, aren't you?"

"No!" answered Boober. His pumpkin hideaway had rolled off, leaving him exposed to the dangers of stampeding pumpkins. "I told you round orange things were bad luck!"

"I want to swim," said Wembley, dodging a pumpkin.

"You can't," sighed Gobo. "The pool's full of pumpkins."

"We'll all be crushed!" shrieked Boober. "I'm getting out of here!" And with that, he disappeared.

"He's always moaning about something," said Red. But she had the nagging suspicion that this time he was right. . . .

7

Trouble in Paradise

"RED, make them stop!" pleaded Mokey. "It's not fun anymore!" The "ahemahemahemahem" sound was deafening.

"But Mokey," argued Red, "you'll never have to go to the Gorgs' Garden again. I did it for you!"

"This is a dream!" cried Mokey desperately. "I have to get you out of it!" And she disappeared behind a giant pumpkin.

Gobo grabbed Red's arm. "Red! This is serious! Look!" He pointed to a pumpkin that had grown so big it almost filled the tunnel. "Only you can stop them!"

"But my Plan! What about my Plan?" cried Red, not wanting to admit to herself that everything was not exactly perfect, and that she might have failed.

Just then Wembley cried out in terror. Red and Gobo turned to see him trapped between two giant pumpkins.

"I can't move!" he screamed.

Red gasped and covered her face. What had gone wrong? Just moments ago it was all so much fun; now her spectacular plan had turned into the scariest nightmare she'd ever had. Everywhere Red looked she saw pumpkins, and she realized at last that she was in a horrible dream. Pumpkins filled the caves and tunnels. Fraggles climbed over them and over each other, trying desperately to escape. Red knew in one explosive flash that the pumpkins could destroy Fraggle Rock; and if they did, it was all her fault. She should never have taken that seed from the Gorgs' Garden—that's where it was supposed to grow, not here in Fraggle Rock. Fraggles didn't know anything about growing vegetables. Anyway, it wasn't meant to be. Pumpkins just didn't belong here.

Through her tears, Red watched Gobo grab Wembley; then everything started to happen in slow motion.

"We're getting out of here!" said Gobo in a strange rubbery voice. "And you better do the same!" He slid through a small gap between a big pumpkin and the wall and disappeared.

"Gobo! Gobo!" Red tried to follow him, but she couldn't get through. "Gobo!" she called again, but her voice was lost in the relentless "ahemahemahemahem" of the pumpkins. Red kicked the nearest one in anger.

Suddenly there was silence.

"The pumpkins!" cried Red. "They've stopped rolling!"

She tried to get out, but she was trapped between two giant pumpkins.

"Help!" she screamed. "I'm trapped!" She listened for an answer, but there was none. All the Fraggles had fled.

Red was having a nightmare and she couldn't wake up.

8
The Great Escape

"NIGHTMARE Alert! Nightmare Alert!" The cry echoed through the tunnels.

Mokey woke with a start. The Fraggle Emergency Siren (consisting of sixteen howling Fraggles, led by Wembley, who could howl the loudest) filled the caves of Fraggle Rock with its warning wail.

Gobo ran into the room, followed closely by Boober. "We all got out!" he reported.

"Except Red," whimpered Boober. He stood by her bed, trembling from hat to socks. They all stared at their friend's nearly motionless body.

"It looks like she's trapped!" said Gobo.

"Trapped in the worst nightmare ever," moaned Boober, who could remember every nightmare ever dreamed. "We've got to get her out of it before she makes it come true!"

For once, no one told Boober to stop worrying. They all knew the power of their dreams—if a dream was dreamed hard enough or long enough, it could come true. And that went for nightmares, too.

So Red's friends instantly got to work trying to wake her up. They shook her, tickled her, massaged her nose. Wembley even howled in her ear. But nothing worked.

Then Mokey was struck with a brilliant idea. "We've got to fill this cave with Fraggles. Quick!" she said. While Gobo and Wembley dragged dazed Fraggles from their beds where they huddled, still trying to block the sight of pumpkins from their minds, Boober and Mokey started blowing up balloons.

Meanwhile, in Red's dream, the pumpkins kept getting bigger and bigger, swelling up like giant blisters.

"I've got to wake up!" cried Red wildly as the bulging pumpkins closed in around her. She frantically pinched herself, slapped her own cheek, and even tried pulling hard on both pigtails at once. Still she remained in her nightmare, surrounded by bloated pumpkins.

Her fear suddenly turned into rage, and Red started to punch a pumpkin. "NO, NO, NO, NO!" she roared, pummeling it with her fists. To her amazement, the pumpkin POPPED! She struck another. POP! And then another—POP! And still more—POP! POP! POP! "I can do it!" she cried, "I can fix it!" And with the force of a tremendous POP!, she blasted herself out of her pumpkin prison and went tumbling through space. The next thing she knew, she was falling . . . falling . . . falling . . .

Pop! Red's eyes popped wide open and she sat bolt upright in bed. All around her stood Fraggles, pins in one hand and limp, broken orange balloons in the other.

"It worked!" said Mokey breathlessly.

"We popped our balloons and popped her back!" cried Gobo. And Red's friends fell on her, laughing and hugging each other.

"Oh, thank goodness! You woke me up and got me out of there!" Red exclaimed when she'd recovered enough from the shock to speak. "Oh, thank you! But before we start to celebrate, I have something important to do."

Red pushed through the happy crowd and dashed down the tunnels toward Pumpkin Cave. Once there, she rushed to the hole she'd dug and found the newly sprouted seed, just as she'd left it. Barely stopping to catch her breath, Red yanked the seed out of the ground, ran back through the dark passageways, past Gobo and Wembley's room, through the Great Hall, and into the tunnel to the Gorgs' Garden.

When she reached the end of the tunnel, she didn't even stop to check for Gorgs. She dashed into the Garden and flung the seed onto the grass. "Get back where you belong!" she shouted and ducked back into the Rock.

"Phase Six," she said, wiping her hands, "forget the whole Plan!"

Red ran back to her room and found her four friends waiting for her. She felt better than she'd felt in days.

"Are you all right?" asked Mokey anxiously. "That was some nightmare!"

They all shuddered.

"Well, I promise you, there's nothing to worry about," said

Red, "because I've just taken that pumpkin seed and dumped it in the Gorgs' Garden where it belongs."

"You mean the part about the seed in the secret cave was really true?" Boober almost fainted from the thought.

"Yes, well . . . I had a Plan. . . ." Red's face felt hot, but before she could get too embarrassed, Gobo reached over and squeezed her arm affectionately. "So your Plan didn't work. Hey Red, what else is new? Listen, think of it this way—it gave us all the liveliest nightmare we've ever had!"

"And we'll thank you not to do it again," said Boober sternly.

"You said it!" agreed Wembley.

"Now, let's swim!" said Gobo.

"Last one in's a fuzzball!" shouted Red, and they bolted out the door.